MAD

MINUTE

MariaLisa deMora

Edited by Hot Tree Editing

First Published 2019

ISBN 13: 978-1-946738-38-7

DEDICATION

*We are made to persist, that's how we find out
who we are. ~ Thomas Wolff*

To those who persevere, holding out a hope for
maybe. I'll always answer your call. You're worth it.

CONTENTS

ACKNOWLEDGMENTS

Each story I write gracefully straddles the wavy line crossing between fact and fiction. I often tease the people around me that every conversation is story fabric for my imagination, mostly because it's true. This book reflects hope I have for so many of my friends, to once again claim their place in the lives of those they love.

Every veteran returning home from a tour of duty, or separating after enlistment shares many truths. In taking up the mantle of service on behalf of the ones left behind, they've set themselves on the path of change. It's inevitable. Something they'll do willingly, painstakingly carving a new identity out of unfamiliar experiences. They color themselves with emotions left-behind friends and family cannot comprehend, and at times glide as a ghost through a world that no longer understands them.

Spend time with someone who served. Ask for their stories. Heed their hidden truths. Be the listening ear when they call in the wee hours, when their spirit is at its darkest, and the need for a guiding light desperate.

Be their courage. It's a worthy task.

Woofully yours,
~ML

Chapter One

Christmas Day

As Kirby Westbrook smiled down at his new girlfriend, Nathan Smith watched his best friend's eyes flash with happiness. The man—not only Nathan's closest friend in the world, but his club president, too—was so in love it was nearly too much to believe, but God, it was good to see. After going through hell on earth, Kirby had managed to reconnect in the best way with someone from his past, a childhood friend he'd secretly had a crush on, and now they were all coupled up.

"You know you're marrying up, right?" Nathan blurted the question, hating himself in the moment, because his soul's sick intent was to strip his friend of even a tiny bit of the happiness shining from his face. Strip it from him with a reminder that relationships came with expectations, and expectations came with the threat of failure, that flawed part of him trusting Kirby'd balk at the reality check. Nathan was contradictorily relieved to see that the look of love Kirby bore only intensified as the thought took hold and dug deep. Yeah, Kirby would clearly be happy to marry Dana, pleased as punch, since right now, right here, the man couldn't imagine a life where he wouldn't be with his woman.

"Good for you," Nathan muttered, taking a step backwards, hiding a wince when he put pressure on his bad leg. *It's a stump*, he reminded himself, as if he could have forgotten. He hadn't had a fucking leg for a long time, and it wasn't like him to forget. The pain, though, that might be enough of a reason. He'd spent too much time in the socket over the past week and was paying for it now. As casually as he could, he leaned an elbow on the counter, taking the weight and strain off the prosthetic.

It felt good but seemed too much like a relief he hadn't earned, so he pushed upright, stoically accepting a resumption of the pain. Pain and exhaustion seemed to be his most loyal companions these days, and Nathan was tired, bone-tired. Sleep was elusive—and more often than not, avoided his stalking efforts completely.

These days, when his body eventually submitted to his dogged demand for rest with his head laid on a pillow, he was the one stalked instead. Dreams chased through his head, through his mind, and tore him loose from the numbing arms of sleep.

Good for you. In the silence of his own head, Nathan infused them with as much hope and prayer as he dared. He shook his head, adjusted his stance again, and watched as Kirby pulled Dana into a close embrace, head dipping until their profiles fused. *You done good, old man.* He pushed off the counter, teetered upright, and tensed all over until he caught his balance, then with gritted teeth left for the media room.

There were ottomans thoughtfully placed in front of every seat, and he positioned himself in front of his favorite chair and toppled backwards into the cushions. The momentum and balance shift flung his leg up, and he held it aloft for a split second before gently bringing it down onto the supportive surface with a stifled groan.

Fuck, it hurts today. Head back, he let his eyes drift closed in the darkened room, willing to let sleep find him here if it would. *Come on, oblivion.* The moment he got comfortable, though, it started, as it always did.

Burning along his shin, the fiery pain wrapped around through his calf and down around the arch of his foot. Heavy pulses of sensation traveled along ghost synapses, driven there by the traumatized nerves in his stump. Agony he could never escape, would never, because it existed in a limb that was ash in the air near a crematory back in Germany. He needed to take off the irritating prosthesis, but the limited relief of pulling the swollen stubbie out of the socket wouldn't be worth the pain it would take to replace it later.

Fucking thing can't let me rest.

He hated it. Hated the amputation that had taken his career, stripped him of one of the only things he'd ever been good at. Hated the loss of mobility, the need to depend on others for so much. The first military-assigned counselor had talked about grieving for the lost limb, and Nathan had outright laughed at him. *"I won't grieve for it. Fuck, at this point, I'd cut the damn thing off myself if it magically grew back."* It had betrayed him, betrayed the natural order of things, considering it just wasn't fucking *there*.

He'd woken in the hospital at Ramstein and had known. Ringing echoes of the blast still sang in his ears, the vision of their vehicle airborne happening over and over against the insides of his closed eyelids. Cutting through the buzz in his head was panic and fear, because he'd known something profound had happened to him. Even flat on his back, he'd felt off-balance somehow, clutching tight to the edges of the mattress, his body convinced it was about to be thrown off and topple to the floor. He'd known, and he'd been afraid to look down, terrified he'd be a full-on cripple, needing a chair for the rest of his life. Nathan had done an inventory, tensed every set of muscles independently, trying to find the missing piece through the mixed signals his body was sending. Hips, thighs, knees, calves, ankles, feet, toes: He'd mapped and located all of them, but it had hurt so damn much. All of it, his everything had ached and throbbed, burning and spearing through him with agony. The pain had been overwhelming, drilling down from his head into his neck, and his damned leg had hurt the worst. That had been what tricked him, making him believe the worst hadn't happened, seeing as if something hurt that badly, it had to still be attached, right?

The moment he'd seen the lopsided drape of the sheet he'd believed. *Warrior no more*. Not accepted. *No, dammit.* He was still the same man inside. But he knew the military wouldn't have a use for him. Didn't matter the surgeon told him it was good news they'd saved his knee, didn't matter the nurses' many and varied messages about how lucky he was to be alive. His fucking leg was gone, brain rattled inside its bonebox, hearing a nonexistent thing, and he'd never walk on his own two feet again.

He'd never serve alongside his brothers-in-arms, his friends, his healthy and whole comrades who were already walking sands he'd never see, having had the bad judgment to catch the blast from an IED without eating it wholesale. *Just my luck*. Taken from the land of war a bloody victor and turned into a piece of meat pitied for no longer being complete, and from then until now, every utterance of sympathy had been like another nail in the coffin of who he used to be.

Old history, moving on. It was time to find something else to think about. If not his military family, then his real one.

Christmas Day. He snorted. Supposed to be the most wonderful time of the year, and he wouldn't get to see or talk to the best part of himself.

Cathy's Law. In his head, he said it like that, imparting his soon-to-be ex-wife's proclamations with mocking status. "Fuck her." *I wish I could fuck her*, his brain immediately supplied, but he squashed the idea.

That was a no-go, something that needed a wave-off from a hot landing zone.

He'd seen her exactly six times since he hit stateside. None of them had been golden moments, and he still couldn't get his head around whatever had happened between stepping on that transport plane to head overseas and the first time he'd seen her head pop into his hospital room at Bethesda Naval. That person hadn't been his Cath, his lover and friend, the woman who completed him in a way he couldn't get past. Losing her had left a hole in his insides, putting him off-balance even more than losing the leg.

Nathan glared at the bare metal of the prosthetic that stuck out beyond the cuff of his pants, only partially hidden by the foot shell and shoe. *Maybe it's the leg.* He blinked, unsuccessful at wishing the metal and plastic monstrosity away. *Or lack of one.* That reasoning didn't seem right, though, because his Cath wouldn't have given a shit. She'd have just been glad to have him back, however that happened. *Well, Cath's gone, and Cathy rules.* Which meant this Christmas, the only thing his little girl—his princess, the light of his life—would get from him was a card with cash in it. No presents, no calls, no visits. It was a shit move on his ex's part, and his lawyer said she couldn't do it, but he knew Cath. Had known Cath. *Cathy.* Nathan shook his head hard to settle his thoughts. His Cath wouldn't do something like this without cause, and hard as it would be, he'd honor it.

Didn't mean he wouldn't be thinking of a certain little five-year-old, though.

Katie.

If she were anything like he'd been as a kid, she'd have been up early this morning. Dancing around the Christmas tree, shouting at the mounds of wrapped presents there. Or maybe there weren't any presents. Maybe that's why Cathy had placed a moratorium on them, if she couldn't afford any and didn't want him to show her up. *Not true.* He reminded himself of the checks he sent every month, over and above what the state took out of his pay from Uncle Sam. *Anything for them.* But unless she was living lavishly, high on the hog, she'd have plenty to take care of her and Katie. What he sent was way more than they'd had any given month as a married couple.

Still married. The thought hurt, surprising him with the wave of pain threaded through with longing. Yes, they were still married, since he was waiting on Cathy to decide she was well and finally done. He wouldn't be the first to make a move. There'd be no flinching from him in this wild game of chicken she'd decided to play.

The sound of the crew in the kitchen grew louder, raucous laughter and teasing helping create unbreakable bonds between the men. Every one of them needed this club, this chance at learning how to fit into the world again. Kirby often said that starting the club, building this foundation, was one of the best things he'd ever done, and Nathan was damn glad his friend had dragged him along for the ride. A thrill of something undefined washed over him, and he grunted when his groin tightened. *What the hell?*

Another crash of phantom pain blasted through his leg, and he hissed as a hand came down on his shoulder. "The fuck you want?" He didn't even turn to see who it was. Truth be told, he couldn't have opened his eyes right now for anyone. Blazing fire licked along those damned phantom nerves until he swore he could feel his toes curling, reaching for any relief to be found.

"Nathan, you got some visitors," Oscar Mayhan told him, the man's gruff East Texas accent distinctive.

"It's fuckin' Christmas Day. Who in the hell would be coming here to the backwoods of bumfuck Texas to visit me?" No way would it be the one woman he wanted to see more than anything, the other half of his heart. Nathan shook his head and shifted in the chair, making himself more comfortable. "Fuck straight off, asshole. I'm not getting back on that damned leg for anybody. Don't wanna see anybody anyway. Just leave me alone."

"Daddy?"

The lone word came from the opening that led to the kitchen, two syllables so soft and uncertain. If he could have bitten his own tongue off, he would have, because if his little girl was here, she'd never be one he didn't want to see. In fact, if his ears weren't deceiving him, this was one of only two people in the world he really *did* want to see today.

"Katie?" Nathan twisted around in the chair so he could look across the room. There, standing in the doorway with the controlled chaos of the club's breakfast behind her, was his little girl. "Oh my God, Katie? Sweet Katie?"

He lurched upright, steadying himself on the back of the chair. The first step he took rocked him with pain so blinding he couldn't see anything. His vision whited out, and he felt himself falling, knee giving way, and there was nothing to catch hold of, Oscar just out of reach, leaving him thundering to the floor. He landed awkwardly and felt something pop, more pain up his leg sending him writhing on the hardwood, crying out.

"Daddy!" Little feet flying his direction had him ducking his head, hiding in shame from his little girl. She could run, and he couldn't even manage to walk across a room without fucking up. Heat covered his cheeks, and she had to be using every muscle in her tiny body to lift his head. Tears in his eyes made everything watery, but he could still see her face. That beautiful sweet face he'd helped make, the face he loved more than life, and it crumpled, falling apart as wet spilled over her lids and down her cheeks. "Daddy, are you hurt? Do you gots a boo-boo?"

He nearly laughed. Only a child would look past the wreck of his body to the immediacy of the fall and consider that the greater of his woes. Nathan stared at her, and she leaned closer until he could smell her scent. The perfume of little-girl happiness: a mix of strawberry shampoo, crisp winter air, evergreens, cocoa, and peppermint all rolled into one. "Yeah," he said, pushing up to a hip so he could flip around, wincing when he tried to straighten his mangled leg. "I got a boo-boo." He reached out and picked her up, tiny bones and tiny body, but a heart larger than any one person had a right to have. *My girl.* He settled her into his lap and drew in the easiest breath in months. "But seeing you fixed me. I'm all fixed, Katie. I missed you, darling girl." He caught sight of Oscar hovering close and shook his head, turning away the offer of help before it was extended. With a frown, Oscar made his way to and through the door, leaving Nathan alone to cuddle the miracle in his lap.

"I can kiss it." She snuggled against him, trusting and sweet, so much a part of him he couldn't imagine how he'd gone all these days without her here. "That'll make it all better. Mommy kisses my boo-boos." She leaned back and clasped his cheeks in her hands again, bright smile searing itself onto his memories for all time. "Oh, I know." She shook his head side to side. "Mommy can kiss it. Her kisses are magic."

Oh, yeah. He knew how magic Cath's kisses were. Years of living for her, with her, he'd studied that lesson every chance he could, acing every test. In the beginning, he'd hold his breath until she'd open the door of the apartment where she'd lived with her best friend, feeling complete only when she leaned into him, face lifted sweetly in invitation for his kisses. He would stand there on the landing and kiss her until her lips were red and swollen, until her neighbor laughingly told them to get a room, until she couldn't catch her breath any more than he could.

He'd known from the first time he'd seen her that Cathy was meant to be his. Meant to be together, that's what he'd told her father when he'd called to ask for her hand. Meant for one another, the preacher had spoken over the rings they'd exchanged standing in the tiny country church her family attended.

Long deployments hadn't been any barrier to what they had. Nathan would walk through the door on his first day of leave and they'd pick back up like nothing had happened. Love and laughter had followed them through the house, hovering over their bed as they took and gave in equal measures. She hadn't been afraid to call him on his bullshit, and he hadn't been afraid to lose her either. They'd been in it for the long haul, laying plans for after his retirement, and she'd known he was a lifer when they wed, supported him without hesitation. She'd whisper her fears in the dark, face buried in his neck, trusting him to keep the pain at bay.

All their plans torn apart by one false step followed by an explosion so loud it had rattled his bones, blown to pieces along with his career, his confidence, and his heart.

"What are you doing here?" He pressed his forehead against Katie's, laughing when she went cross-eyed trying to focus on him. "I didn't expect to see you, Katie-bug."

"Mommy said it was a surprise." She chewed on her bottom lip, eyes ringed with white. "Are you surprised, Daddy?"

"Oh, yeah. Very surprised." He stared at her in awe for a moment, floored by the fact she was here, now, when he'd just been wishing for something exactly this. *How the hell did this come about?* "It's a good surprise."

"The best." Katie nodded fast, then rolled her eyes as she pretended to be dizzy while he held her steady. "I missed you, Daddy. You moved a long way away."

"I know." Nathan swallowed hard. "I had to."

Her voice dropped to a bare whisper. "Mommy said you had to, too. Said you couldn't get better at our house. Why, Daddy? Why did you have to go?" Chin quivering, she bared her pain when she asked in a tear-thickened voice, "Why?"

Yeah, Nathan, why? Things that had seemed so crystal-clear months ago now were muddy and dark, clarity lost in the pain-filled interim. Days spent missing his family, his job, while every long night was grief-filled because he was missing his *whole* life. Those times that came before he'd been wrecked and left on the side of the pathway, parts torn from him until he was a bloody mess, inside and out.

"You remember the hospital?" Piss-scented hallways, sleepless nights spent fighting the pain, the feeling of desperation carried into the morning's bleak sunrise by a steady tide of groans and shouts of anger. He'd hated the times Cath had brought Katie to see him, because he hadn't wanted that to become a memory for her. Not one associated with her daddy, the man who'd stood tall and proud, who'd flown her superhero-style over his head, who'd banished the monsters from her closet. He remembered it only too well, had been glad to see the last of that place. "They did all they could to help Daddy." She scrunched up her nose, and he nodded. "Yeah, they couldn't make it better, so Daddy had to find someone who could help him."

That someone had been Kirby, a brother even before he'd offered Nathan his patch. Nathan had never been part of an MC before, had only ridden along the fringes on charity runs, but he'd been envious of the connection those men had. Then there'd been Kirby, holding out hope for a kind of camaraderie Nathan had been missing, longing for. He'd been willing to take on someone like Nathan, crippled and useless, and who was Nathan to say no? He'd jumped at the chance, then found out all the other pieces Kirby wanted to do, which only made it an even more attractive offer.

"Did you? Did you find someone? Are you coming home now?"

A woman's voice in the other room saved him from answering, and he looked up in time to see Cathy walk into view, head turned to the side as she chatted with Oscar, who was no doubt bringing her in here next.

"Mommy." Katie bounced on his thighs, and Nathan suppressed a pained groan as the socket twisted. "Mommy, Mommy, Mommy. I found Daddy."

Chapter Two
Cathy

"Hey, Cathy. Check it out. She found him." Oscar tipped his head towards an open doorway where Katie had disappeared a few seconds ago. It was darker in that room than this, so it took Cathy's eyes a moment to adjust. Then she saw them. Saw *him*.

She had loved Nathan almost from the first time she'd met him. A laughing, boasting, handsome, larger-than-life man occupying a booth in her section of the little hometown diner where she'd worked summers. He'd been seated with his friends, talking about some pickup basketball game they'd just won, and he'd jokingly accepted accolades and shaken his head even as they embellished each story, enlarging his part in every play that took the team to the win. It was all in jest, of course, and in reality, as she'd come to know him well,

Nathan turned out to be one of the most modest men she'd ever met.

Humble but driven, and due to that trait, borne along by a deep confidence in his own abilities. He'd talked about all the things he'd wanted to do, moving to a stool at the counter long after his friends had gone home. Drinking cup after cup of coffee as an excuse to stay and talk, and talk. And listen, since eventually, he'd asked enough leading questions to get her over her shyness.

Nathan had walked her home that night, pestering until he had not only her phone number but her schedule for the next two weeks. He'd appeared back at the door the next morning with a box of pastries in hand and waltzed past her best friend, up the hallway, and into her bedroom to give her the kind of sweet wake-up call all women dreamed of. A week later, knowing she'd gone home for a visit, he'd talked his way into her parents' home and, by the time she'd made it downstairs, had been ensconced in the kitchen with a mug of coffee in hand, avidly listening to her father's stories about his days in the military.

When Nathan had decided to enlist, she hadn't opposed the idea. Although they'd been dating for months, they were not yet married and she'd held her tongue. They'd been seated in the back row at a movie when he'd turned to her in the theater, eyes shining in eagerness after watching a video advertisement during the previews, and said, "I'm gonna do it," and she hadn't told him no. Even having heard dozens of her mother's stories to lend a sense of caution to her own excitement, because the life of a military spouse was far from glamorous, she hadn't told him no.

His first call home during basic scared her. He'd sounded so beaten, exhausted in a way she'd never heard him, and yet there had still been that drive to compete, to be better. The next call had been different, cautiously confident in his abilities, and promising her the world if she'd just stick with him. Graduation had been the game changer, when unbeknownst to her, he'd already talked to her father. So when he got down on one knee in the middle of the field full of men in uniforms just like his, her dad had been the one handing him a ring to place on her finger.

They'd had a quick wedding, more easily accomplished than she'd expected, and as simply as that, she'd become Mrs. Nathan Smith. A week later she'd been holding his hand through the window of a bus, feeling empty and lost when their grip finally slipped, the bus gaining speed and leaving her standing at the side of the road in a cloud of exhaust and exhaustion.

The first of many separations through the years, him stationed temporarily in locations that only offered provisional family housing or deployed into the war zones of the Middle East. Mission-oriented, those camps weren't pseudo towns where the men and women could bring family, which meant their frequent video chats were even more of a lifeline to her. She'd never asked him to give it up, not when it was good and not when it was tough. Even after they had Katie, she'd held firm on following the path they had laid out together as a family. She worked, had gotten a business degree, managed their home and her career, and loved her husband enough to hold tight to what they had.

Cathy didn't know if he understood how she'd found out he was injured, if he'd learned of the delay in notification. Her first indication of something gone wrong was his missed chat. One virtual date passed, then another, and when she'd reached out to women who had husbands in the same unit, they'd only known there were losses but no names. Every car door slam outside their house had her on edge, waiting for the notification she dreaded with every fiber of her being. Days and days of limbo, every nerve stretched thin, shielding Katie from everything as much as she could.

When it had finally come, the news had been good. "He's alive but injured and being transferred stateside for treatment."

That was when the real nightmare began.

The first visit had been a disaster, Katie too excited about seeing Daddy, Cathy too nervous, and Nathan too angry. His shouted curses heard from down the hallway had been her first warning, the rolled eyes of an orderly her second. Still, she'd persisted, wanting—no, needing—to see her husband for herself, to verify he was alive and breathing. She'd rounded the open door with Katie in her arms just in time to see Nathan throw a table towards the window, where it bounced off ineffectually. His scream of anger pierced the fog she'd been in since receiving the phone call, and she'd cradled Katie's head to her shoulder as she waited for him to see them.

Head back, neck straining with the force of his yell, he'd finally turned to look towards the door where she stood, their daughter in her arms. Red-faced, veins bulging at his temples, he'd lifted clenched fists and pounded the sides of his face as he screamed for her to leave. "Get out," he yelled. "Get out, get out, getout, getoutgetout." Over and over, he'd shouted at her, reverberations of his rage echoing through the room, her body shaking with the impact of his fury. Far from the loving reunion she'd hoped for, he'd rejected her and their life—and when Katie, tiny sweet Katie, asked who the angry man was, Cathy had fled.

Subsequent visits had been better, but that was a relative term, and for the first time in her life with Nathan, Cathy hadn't known what to do. She couldn't fix this, couldn't help him, couldn't make it better. He seemed to know what he wanted, the entirety of which was her *gone*, something that was at odds with the loving and gentle man her husband had always been. He'd remained adamant, seated firmly in his rejection of their life, and finally, not knowing what else to do, she'd taken a step back and waited, hoping he'd come to a different conclusion eventually.

He hadn't, and before she'd known what was happening, he'd been gone, separated from the military that had been his home for so long, and from her and Katie, the people he'd once said he loved more than breath. A change of address card was the only warning that he didn't see himself coming home.

It had taken months until Cathy understood through long conversations with a counselor provided by the military, but finally, she got it. While she was no less angry at Nathan now than she'd been in the beginning, she at least tried to understand why he'd pushed them away. Why he'd demanded space to learn how life fit around him in this new shape.

In her mind, he'd had enough time. She was here in the middle of nowhere Texas because she was on a mission. It was time to get her family back.

She stared through the door at the cluster of bodies on the floor, Nathan seated with legs extended, Katie in his lap, cuddled close and holding on with all the strength in her tiny arms. He wasn't yelling, wasn't screaming at them to go, and that felt like a win. Katie called out happily, and Cathy held her breath as Nathan's gaze caught hers. Then the light in his eyes faded, his features set in harsh lines, and he lifted Katie from his lap, settling her feet on the floor.

"Go to Momma, Katie-bug." Nathan bent over and fiddled with something on his leg, then looked up at Katie, who hadn't moved, staring down at him. "Don't stare." Voice roughened with some emotion, he shook his head. "Stop it. It's not polite to look at cripples." Katie stayed where she was, gaze fixed on her father's face. It looked like an attempt to hide when he angled his head down again and continued to fuss with whatever it was. "Oscar, brother." Warmth in his voice was surprising after he'd just been cool to Katie. "Gonna need some sticks. I jacked the leg up when I fell."

"Damn, man. Want me to get your other leg?" Oscar walked towards Nathan and stooped by his legs, reaching out to run his fingers over the same place Nathan had been working with. "Let me get you off the floor at least."

"No." Nathan shook his head. "I can manage."

"Yeah, you can. Don't mean you have to." Oscar glanced up at Katie, who still stood beside Nathan's shoulder. "Wanna help your daddy with me?" Her little girl looked at Cathy, who nodded encouragingly. "Okay, you pull up on his arm there, and we'll get him off the floor."

"Daddy?" Katie's voice trembled, and she scooted a half step away. "What's wrong?"

"Daddy's leg got hurt, Katie bug." Cathy held tight to the doorframe, afraid to move towards them. If Nathan rejected her again, here, today, she didn't know if she could fit the pieces together again. "We talked about that. I told you how part of his leg is gone, and now he gets to use a robot leg to help him walk."

"He fell down." Katie was staring at her, and Cathy was glad, as it meant their little girl didn't see the pain and anger that swept over Nathan's face. "Why did he fall down? He got a boo-boo, Momma. I said you'd kiss it better."

"Let's get you up, brother." Oscar stood over Nathan and dragged an ottoman closer. "On three." He bent and gripped Nathan's belt, working his fingers around the stout leather. Nathan rested his hands on Oscar's shoulders. "One," she could see Nathan's muscles tense, "two," Oscar set his feet firmly, "three," he lifted, and Nathan's good leg bent, getting underneath himself as best he could as Oscar pivoted until Nathan sat on the ottoman.

"Leg's borked, bro." Nathan shoved Oscar's hands away. "Leave it. I want it on for now. Fuckin' leave it."

"Ohhhh. Daddy said a bad word." Katie giggled. "Mommy says even if Donny says that word, I can't. Donny says his mommy uses it all the time. He told me she never stops using it. Mommy, did you hear Daddy?"

The cool façade of Nathan's expression cracked the tiniest amount, and Cathy met his eyes over their daughter's head. Katie remained happily chattering away about the little boy at her preschool who got in trouble a lot about his language. Everything faded to the background, Oscar fussing around Nathan's legs, Katie swinging on his arm as she yanked and tried to get his attention. Nathan's gaze held everything Cathy had hoped to see. Love and hope, even if it was tempered by sadness and pain. He wasn't unhappy to see them, and any guilt she'd felt at her subterfuge over Christmas fell away.

I have a week to make this work.

She stared into the eyes of the only man she'd ever loved and said a prayer.

It has to work.

21

Chapter Three
Nathan

"You knew she was comin'." He kept his tone even, forcing down his anger and hurt that his friend would ambush him in this way. "You listened to me bitch and moan about not being allowed to go and see my little girl, and let me carry on and on, knowing the whole time that Cathy was comin' here."

Cathy had taken Katie to the bathroom. The shift in his daughter's demeanor had been abrupt, going from loving on him to being afraid of him, to laughing hysterically about his "bad word" slipup, and finally to jumping on one leg while screeching that she "had to go." As she had with everything in their lives together, Cathy had taken it all in stride, managing Katie's excitement in an unfamiliar place while surrounded by evidence of the life he was making without them. Wasn't much of a life, he knew, but the men here had his back, no questions asked.

Except apparently Oscar, who was a traitor of the highest order.

"Got that right. I knew it and didn't say a damn word." Oscar nodded with a sour grin. "You'd'a told her no."

"Damn right I would have. I don't need them to see me like this." He gestured towards the floor. "When my little girl's runnin' at me to be picked up, and I fall on my ass? I fall on my ass, right in front of her. Brother, that's not how I want her to remember me."

"But you want her to remember you, right?" Oscar paused in the doorway. "Because to have her remember you, that means you gotta be around. Think on that a minute, brother. I'm going to get your crutches. Be right back."

Nathan grimaced as he watched Oscar walk out of sight. *Be right back.*

That could be a tagline for his life these days. People moving around him all the time, leaving him stuck on an island in the middle of a stream that was his life. He hated being dependent on anyone, had always been the guy others turned to when they had problems. The friend they leaned on when they needed something, anything. He'd twist himself into knots to try and help those he loved, and he knew it wasn't rational, but he had never expected others to do the same for him.

Men in the field learned to trust and depend on each other, sure. Mutual survival demanded that kind of interwoven responsibility to ensure a cohesive unit. He'd never had a problem with that on missions, or even training for a mission. Learning each other's strengths and weaknesses simply meant you'd all work in lockstep together, lifting each other up and over whatever barrier or wall there was. Brotherhood in its purest form, and something that felt nearly like a religion at times. He'd known men who didn't do well on leave, since they felt like they were missing a piece of themselves. A third leg or arm that wasn't necessary for day-to-day living but had become so much a part of their daily fabric that just being away lent an undefined sense of unease.

He'd lost that third leg, and part of a second one, and what was left? Not enough to stand on.

Pain rippled up from his toes through the calf, into the stubbie and up to his hip, nerves firing in spontaneous patterns of agony. Nathan closed his eyes and rode out the discomfort, holding his breath for a five-count before blowing it out slowly. He kept that cycle for a few long moments, trying to force some semblance of control into place.

"Does it hurt much? Katie said you fell, Nathan. Are you okay?" Cathy's voice was soft and close, and he looked up at her standing in front of him, crutches clutched to her.

The concern on her face tore at something in his chest, an oozing wound gained when he lost the leg, lost his place on his squad, lost his place in the world, and he froze at the feeling. *She almost looks like she still—* He cut off the thought viciously, shoving the idea to the side with enough effort maybe it wouldn't come back to haunt him.

"Nathan…I—"

"I'm fine." He kept his voice deliberately clipped and curt, and after delivering those two words, watched her waver on her feet, as if hit with the concussive wave from an explosion.

"Are you mad at me?"

He stared at her, seeing the telltale indications of her nervousness. Nose wrinkled in that too-cute way she had, something Katie had inherited from her, lips reddened and puffy from being raked between her teeth, an action she performed again just now. He suppressed a groan because that was one of his favorite things to do when he kissed her.

Cathy had always gone crazy when he'd kissed her rough, hard, owning her mouth. From the first time they'd loved on each other, lying together in a rented hotel bed since her roommate was a nosy woman and he hadn't wanted Cathy to deal with anything from her, best friends or not, he'd taken lead in their lovemaking. She hadn't been innocent—and hadn't that played on his mind for a long time, imagining her comparing him to that nameless, faceless man in her past, the only other one she'd been with. Not innocent, but near enough that he'd gotten to introduce her to all the joys of carnal delights. College had been a time of exploration for him, and he'd been lucky enough to land with an older woman, him a freshman and her a senior, and now, thinking about it, didn't that mean he and Cathy had the same experiences, really? At least until he'd left her high and dry at home, waltzing away on his one leg to Texas. Who was to say she hadn't been with a dozen men since, all of them better than he was in the sack, all of them whole and uncrippled, and all of them a better fit for her? A partner who would walk at her side, not limp along behind.

"Nathan?" Red flagged her cheeks, and he realized he'd been staring at her this whole time, silent, sounds of the holiday gathering continuing on in the distant kitchen, Katie's laughter winding through the house as the men he'd thrown his lot in with took care of her.

"No, I'm not mad at you." He wasn't, he realized. Not anymore. There'd been a moment of white-hot fury when he'd embarrassed himself by falling in front of his little girl, but Cathy hadn't seen, at least. "Not at you, Cath." He forced a smile, hating how it felt on his face, fake and plastic, sitting uneasily on top of the muscles and skin like an ill-fitting Halloween mask, limiting visibility and only working to frustrate the wearer. "Never at you." The words were true even if the smile was fake.

"Oscar said you need these?" She transferred the crutches to one hand, lifting the other to wipe at the corner of her eye. "What happened?"

And just like that, the anger was back along with the smells of that street in Afghanistan, the sounds of the creaking transport idling up the center of the road with gravel crunching underneath the tires. He walked to one side, scanning the road ahead and peering into the darkened ruins on either side of them. Another man walked point on the other side of the road, and he couldn't remember his name for a moment, shaking his head until it came back to him. "Bowman. That's it. Bowman."

"What?" Cathy sounded confused, and why wouldn't she be? She couldn't see what he did.

"Bowman died."

The blast came from that side, a delayed trip trigger that let the men on foot get twenty feet beyond before it detonated, just beside the Stryker carrying six men. The vehicle flipped into the air, and Nathan watched analytically as it sailed, graceful as a leaping dancer ghosting through the clouds of dirt and rock. It shouldn't be aerodynamic—the light armored vehicle was a lumbering beast at best—but as it took flight and twisted through the air, it nearly looked like it could fly. He lost the ability to breathe, body blown backwards against a mostly intact wall of the building behind him, air knocked loose as his hands lifted in an ineffectual warding off motion that did nothing to keep the front edge of the vehicle from shearing off his leg as it pinned him in place. Stuck like a bug on a board, wings still fluttering as the metal speared through.

"Nathan?"

Cathy's voice was wrong. She shouldn't be there. She wasn't deployed, walking down a dusty street in Syria. She was home doing the hard work, making sure their daughter was safe and happy and well and knew she was loved. She talked about Nathan to Katie all the time, making him part of each day, so that when he came home on leave, he fit right back in as if he'd always been there. That was a talent she had, a skill so subtle and goddamned needed that he couldn't define it. He just needed it. Needed to know he was part of more than that group of men he worked and lived and bled with. Needed to know there was love waiting at home for him.

"Nathan?"

"I'm here." He shook his head, and the overwhelming memories receded. They'd be back, he knew. They always came back. "I'm here."

"Nathan."

He blinked. She was closer, and the heat against his cheek was her hand, not blood, not the rough scores from the hundred-mile-an-hour stones that had left furrows and scars behind. Her hand, her palm, her fingers, all so well known, and yet entirely foreign. He could feel the trembling as she touched him, fear and nerves, and she'd been like that the first time, too.

Hair spread on the pillow, Cathy had looked up at him, eyes liquid pools of desire as he touched her. Sheet pulled to their shoulders because the room was cold, something they'd laughed about as he'd undressed her. "I'll warm you up, baby," he'd cheesed, easing her shirt off her shoulders and seeing goose bumps covering her skin. She'd laughed and cupped his cheek before raising her head for a kiss.

Mouth to her ear, he asked permission. "I wanna touch you." She moved underneath the sheet, hand running down his arm until her fingers twisted with his. She brought his palm to her breast and sighed when he kneaded her flesh gently. "You're so beautiful, Cath. I'll take care of you."

He pushed up on an elbow and stared down at her. Gorgeous in her passion, she looked up with half-hooded eyes. He shifted to lie between her thighs, and Cathy's lips parted on a soft moan as her hips rocked up to meet him. "I want you." She gave him a tiny grin. "If you'll have me."

"Oh, I'll have you, woman." He reached between them and lined himself up with her entrance. "I'll have all of you." Her eyes widened as he slid inside, a slow, steady glide that left him gasping for breath. "God, Cath. You feel so good." Tight and hot, the sleek muscles of her core clutched at him, pulling him deeper. "So goddamned good."

He told her the truth. "I love you." No "still," no "always," and he hoped she understood what he meant. He'd never stopped loving her, never needed those kinds of modifiers to quantify the timing of that love.

She blinked slowly, looking shocked; then her eyes closed as something he hoped was relief washed over her face.

"I'm not mad, Cath. Promise." He reached and took one of the crutches, holding it upright at his side. His other hand covered hers, pressing her palm tighter against his skin.

They stayed like that for a moment, breathing and just being together. Then Katie's excited shout rang through the room as she ran back in. "Mommy, Mommy. There's gonna be a Jesus cake and then *presents!*"

Cathy pulled back, and her hand fell away, Nathan missing the heat and touch immediately. He'd always been that way with her. Needing more and more, and Cathy had always given him what he needed. He knew if he asked for it right now, she'd turn back to him and hold him.

God, how can I be so back and forth with this shit? One moment he was pissed, furious at her for withholding Christmas from him. Then he was angry that she was here and giving him a Christmas he didn't deserve. With one breath he loved and missed her, and the next he was embedded back with his squad as they lay dying on the road. *PTSD,* he thought, that catch-all explanation annoying. Concussions played into it, too, and his unresolved feelings about the amputation. This was what he'd wanted to spare her, the things the counselor had advised him would happen, the things he would feel, and how his emotions could shift and swing on a dime. *I didn't want her to see this.*

Cathy crouched until she was Katie's height, one knee to the floor as she listened to their daughter's excited explanation about what a Jesus cake was.

"Where are you staying?" *Not here, please God, not here.* Where that thought had come from he didn't know.

"In a house a couple of blocks over. Oscar set us up." Her response was quick and reassuring, laying his terror momentarily to rest. She swiveled to face him. "I'd ask if you wanted to see it, but I parked the car there." She seemed to realize she still held one of the crutches. "Oh, sorry." Standing was a fluid movement for her, a grace he'd never manage again, every motion now a mix of stillness and surges of strength as one leg tried to do the work meant for two. One stride and she was in front of him, holding out the promised support. "You probably don't want to—" She cut off her words abruptly, embarrassment staining her face red.

"I can manage at least a couple of blocks on the sticks. And if I couldn't—" He angled the crutches to help himself upright, quietly noting the aborted movement she made as she stopped herself from trying to help. Most wouldn't have curbed that instinct and could have toppled him all over again. She either didn't trust herself to help or trusted him to handle the movement. Either way, it was interesting to see. "Then, the club has a van for transport as needed. We could borrow that." He shoved the cushioned bars underneath his arms, wincing at the lightning fast flicker of pain when they struck the constantly irritated nerve bundle there. Between months spent on crutches and ill-fitting lifting belts, his brachial nerves were always ready to flare up. *Just another day in the life.* "But first, we need to see if the Jesus cake is ready, right, Katie?"

His little girl stared up at him, expression serious and somber as she watched him maneuver the crutches to stand beside Cathy. Then the clouds broke and the sun shone through, her smile beaming up at him. "You are so tall, Daddy. When did you get so tall?"

"I've been this size a while, darlin'." He returned her smile, laughing when she came to stand right in front of him, head tipped far back. "You're the one who's grown. I think you're half a foot taller now."

She lifted one shoe and looked at it, then down at his feet, clearly measuring the difference. "Your foot or mine?"

"Oh, definitely mine. You're such a big girl." Crutches wedged into place, he lifted a hand to her head, ruffling her hair. "Still my girl, right?"

"Always, Daddy." Katie eyed the crutches distrustfully. "Will those keep you from falling again?"

"That's the idea, punkin. My leg needs fixin', but that'd take me away from you for a while today. I'd rather be with you, so I'll be on these until then." He had another leg, but it was a different model, newer and theoretically better, and he hadn't gotten the hang of it yet. Nerve-driven rather than gravity, it moved differently from the one he'd become accustomed to over the months. The physiotherapist said he needed to trust it, but Nathan was happier without change these days.

"Oh, we're here for long days. I can help you, Daddy." She moved to stand beside him and put both hands on the struts of the crutch. "Tell me when and I'll help you."

"When," he said, wanting to see what she'd do. With a grunt and a heave, she yanked on the crutch, trying to shift it forwards. He moved his weight off and let her get it positioned. "That's helpful."

"I know." She looked up at him with that damn smile again, and it felt as if a thousand pounds had lifted off him in the past two minutes alone. *At this rate, I'll be soaring anytime now.* "I'm a good helper. Mommy says."

"Well, Mommy's not wrong." He looked up to see Cathy wiping at one corner of her eye again, sniffing suspiciously. "Cath?"

"It's just good to see you, Nathan." She gestured towards him and Katie. "Good to see this."

He'd done that, taken not only her husband away, but also the father of their daughter. Gone and left her to deal with everything alone. That realization struck him hard, and within the next breath, he turned a corner from where he'd been just this morning. They'd always been a team, and he'd struck out on his own without explanation. He'd found that while he could go it alone, he didn't like it. *No more*, he vowed.

This morning he'd been angry and bitter, facing the specter of Christmas without his family. Now, he was standing here in front of his wife, whom he loved more than life, with their little girl huffing and tugging at his crutch in an effort to help out any way she could.

I've been an idiot.

He just hoped it wasn't too late to fix everything he'd been so determined to break.

Chapter Four
Cathy

The kitchen was controlled chaos, and Cathy looked around for the woman she'd met earlier, Dana. Manager of the organization that was the foundation behind the motorcycle club, the woman had been nearly as determined as Oscar to get Cathy and Katie here today.

In the back of her mind, she'd had an idea of how this clubhouse would look, but reality was nothing like her imagination had filled in on their trip to Texas, during those long hours with nothing to do except talk to a five-year-old or think. So much thinking, and her overwhelmed nerves nearly had her turning around a dozen times. All her imagining and yet nothing could have prepared her for the sight of a dozen men leaning together over a waist-high island, arguing over the best recipe for pancakes.

Katie continued to chatter to Nathan as they moved slowly behind her. Cathy was confident he would have been faster on his own, but the look on his face when Katie had set her jaw shouted that their daughter still had her daddy wrapped around even her littlest finger. If it made her happy to pretend to help him move one slow crutch-step at a time, he would have turned himself inside out to make that happen.

Maybe there is hope.

It felt like so long since she'd held any optimism about him, about them, but today Nathan had said the words, those words he'd always held so close to the chest, the ones that set her flying like a balloon.

"You look like you need a job to do."

Cathy turned at the gruff words and looked up at a man she scarcely recognized. With a cry, she fell into his open arms, wrapping hers around his waist.

"Do not bawl, woman."

Sniffing, she shook her head back and forth. "Not bawling. Someone's cookin' onions somewhere. That's all."

"How you doin', Cath?" Kirby Westbrook had been deployed with Nathan for a long time, and when they were stateside, the bachelor had spent more of his leave hanging out at their house than in his own quarters, and she'd been forever happy to host him. She'd known part of it was a desire to not have to face his demons alone, because both men came home from every deployment changed. It killed her having to watch them claw their way back to a semblance of normal bit by bit, topping the hill of nerves and anger until finally they were coasting down the backside of peaceful and happy, just before being sent back overseas. So when being with a family helped Kirby to deal with whatever he and Nathan saw or did that made their faces so haunted, she'd been honored to open their home to him.

"You look good." She sidestepped his question deftly, not wanting to break down for real. So many emotions swirled through her that she couldn't find a way to talk about any of it without going against his decree about crying. "Did you see Katie yet?"

"Not to speak. Not yet." He pulled back and smiled down at her. "Little bug looks to have her hands full with Daddy."

Cathy tipped her head as she stared into his face. Lines were far less pronounced than the last time she'd seen him, and there was an ease to his stance that said even in the crowded room, he was comfortable. "Something good has happened to you."

Grin widening, he flashed a glance towards the chestnut-haired woman standing near the stove. "I kinda got hit by a truck."

"Excuse me?" If getting hit by a truck was good, she wasn't sure she could handle the bad.

He gestured down to where his socked foot dangled just above the floor, something she hadn't noticed until now. "Yeah, I kinda got hit by a truck, but it's the best thing that could have happened. Swear." A shadow eclipsed the joy on his face for an instant, then was gone. "Concussed again, but not bad. And it was so, so worth it."

"When? Are you sure you're okay?" Fear struck her like a blow. *Oh, no*. Repeated concussions could be deadly. She knew since she'd done the research after discovering the many TBI incidents Nathan had suffered. Most of which he'd hidden from her, as they'd happened overseas and by the time he'd cycled home he just hadn't mentioned them. But with his injury, the amputation and additional surgeries, his whole medical history had been laid out for her by his surgeons. Terrified wasn't a strong enough word to cover her emotions at finding out about all his near-miss events through the years. No wonder the men always looked haunted when they came back. They'd just spent however many months wandering through a landscape rife with danger, where an enemy waited around every corner, and death could come raining down from the sky at any moment.

"Yeah, I'm good. Leg's bunged up a bit." He gestured to a pair of crutches leaning against the countertop. "But nothing that won't heal." He took a mug down and filled it with coffee, holding it out to her.

His confidence helped ease her fears, and she accepted the heat and weight of the cup, cradling it against her chest for a moment before leaning back as she sipped. "So how did you get hit? Were you riding?" She put a hand on his arm and crowded forwards, asking pseudo-seriously, "Is the bike okay? Did she survive?"

His laughter was good to hear, and she watched him rock backwards with his amusement, chin lifted as he shouted out towards the ceiling. Movement then heat beside her hit with a déjà vu so strong she felt the hairs on the back of her neck lift in a wave.

Nathan was propped against the countertop right beside her, crutches handed off to Katie, who was now walking around the room with them, arms thrust between the struts down near the bottom, cushioned armrests reaching far over her head like a stork's wings. Cathy smiled at the reminder of summertime fun, using stilts when she was a child, posing challenges with friends for most steps without falling or fastest ten-yard dash.

The heat of him grew, and her breath stopped in her throat when, in a move that echoed far back into the past, Nathan slipped an arm around her back, fingers threading through a belt loop to tug her sideways against his body.

"Got another mug of joe?" Even before Nathan finished the question, Kirby had brought another coffee cup out and filled it. Nathan claimed it from him and lifted the mug to his mouth for a sip. "He tell you about his little accident?"

"I was just startin' to when you so rudely interrupted." Kirby's grin took any heat from the words. "She seemed to be more worried about the bike than me."

"You weren't even on the bike." Nathan shook his head. "Man was wanderin' through traffic like an idiot and got himself run over."

"Oh my God." Cathy looked back at Kirby to see a fond expression on his face. "You really *did* get hit by a truck?"

"There were extenuating circumstances." He cupped a hand around his mouth and called across the room. "Dana, why did I get hit by a truck again?"

To Cathy's surprise, the woman blushed red as a beet before she turned her back to them and busied herself with something on the stovetop. Her words were addressed to the cabinets as she responded, "I don't know, Kirby Westbrook, but I'm sure with you, there's a story involved."

"You guys are together." The words slipped from Cathy without her conscious approval, but when Nathan chuckled, she knew she was on point. "You and Dana? That's awesome. I like her."

"How do you know her?" Nathan deflected her attention back to him. "You just met her, right?"

"We've talked on the phone a couple of times." Cathy downplayed the amount of planning that had gone into getting her and Katie here today. "She seems really nice."

"She is nice." He raised his voice much as Kirby had. "Except when she's stickin' her nose into business that isn't hers."

From the doorway, Oscar chimed in, "Don't complain when it got you the Christmas present you wanted most in the world." The whole scene was so damn homey. These men, joking and jostling for space along the prep area, picking on each other with such comfort and ease, felt just like an extended family. The respect and caring were apparent with every interaction, and the way they'd folded her and Katie into their holiday morning said so much about all of them.

"I like what you've got here." She waited a beat, but Nathan didn't respond, so she lifted her mug in a tiny salute. "I understand now why you wanted this. I'm happy for you, Nathan. You deserve to have good friends like these."

"Brothers." He shrugged, but his fingers dug a little deeper into her side, holding on tighter. "They're my brothers. That's what club means, you know?"

"Like the squad." She understood that, having presided over more than one barbecue where the unspoken conversations had rung as loudly as the spoken ones, where she could watch the wheel and turn of the group as they moved through a crowd, always aware of the presence and position of the other men they trusted and depended on. "That makes sense. Like I said—" She drained her mug and set it on the counter beside her hip. "I'm happy for you."

"But." He'd tensed up, muscles ringing with strain as he prepared for something she didn't understand.

"But what?" She noticed Katie had crutched her way over to where Oscar stood and was peering up, talking to him. "No buts, I'm just happy for you."

"It's a long way from the coast."

Ah. Now she understood where he was coming from with his apprehension. Maybe Nathan didn't remember, but she'd been willing to follow him base-to-base through his career, and they'd had no less than seven different housing assignments on the various bases.

He eyed his coffee for a moment. "Not a place to raise a family."

"Not this building, no." The little home Oscar had settled her and Katie in was far better suited for the intimacy needed in a relationship. A marriage. A team to put back together, so the challenges could be more equally shared. She shrugged. "Plenty of other houses in Mayhan."

"Are you for real, Cath?" The hopeful look in his eyes eased the grip fear had on her heart. "I wasn't kind." The noise in the kitchen and dining area had grown subdued, and she knew the men were all listening in, part of the defense of the group to ensure they knew what was gong on with one of their own. That way they could help Nathan get past whatever rejection he seemed so certain was coming. "Not at all. I was a dick to you."

She turned to him, needing to see his face as he listened to what she had to say. *I didn't plan on an audience like this.* It didn't matter. Nathan needed to hear it, and if he wanted to do this here, thinking maybe his little troop of onlookers would keep her from saying what was in her heart, then he would get it here, both barrels.

Chapter Five
Nathan

He watched the expression on Cathy's face change, hardening into a mask he didn't recognize, didn't like. *I did that. I changed her.* Echoes of his shouted insults rang through his head, and he cringed inside. He'd been such an ass to her, trying hard to drive her away, because he hadn't felt worthy of a woman like her. Whole, loving, with so much potential. He'd been convinced it would be better for her if he dropped from her life entirely and let her move on with someone else. Someone not crippled, not chased by demons every moment of the day.

"When you—"

"Wait, before you—" He butted in before she had a chance to say anything, giving her words that were inadequate and small, but all he had. Setting his mug down, he fumbled for her hand, the left one, the one that had made her his all those years ago, he blurted, "I need you to know I'm sorry."

"Sorry?" Her voice rose on the end of the word, until the sound lashed through the air like a whip. "You're sorry?"

"Yeah. I didn't do right by you." Hands shaking, he tightened his hold, trying to hide the reaction from Cathy. She hadn't moved out of his grip, so he anchored himself with the feel of her under his palm, heat and flesh, the body of the woman he loved, a body he knew so well. Memorized every inch of her with touch, caresses, and love.

"No, you didn't. You need me to know you're sorry?"

He nodded, since those words meant at least she'd heard him. Even if she turned and walked out right now, he'd know she'd heard him and understood a small part of what he'd wanted to say.

"Well, I need you to know a couple of things, too. You ready to listen to me?" Her jaw firmed as she waited for his response, chin jutting forwards in that expression her father had called the "oh shit" look. That was the same look little Katie had given him not ten minutes ago as she'd made clear her determination to help him walk with the crutches.

"Yeah, Cath. I'm ready."

"Fuckin' finally," Kirby muttered as he turned away, facing the coffeemaker.

"You were the worst kind of jerk, and I hated you for a hot minute." Her words cut so deep it was a wonder he wasn't bleeding out. "You made me doubt my role, my place in your life. Made me doubt the things I knew about you, because you weren't the same man." She shook her head. "I'd never seen you mean, but, Nathan, you crafted words like weapons and aimed them right at me, and that..." She pulled in a breath and he felt every suppressed sob as her chest hitched. "That hurt more than you will ever know. You knew all my weakest points and attacked them ruthlessly. Every time I saw you in the hospital, you pulled the rug out from under me and laid me out. Then you took away even that when you told them I couldn't see you anymore. You barred me from bringing our daughter to see you, banned me from your presence without a word of explanation to me."

He barely remembered those days; they had become a muddle of dark memories, lost hours of deadly impulses twisting inside him until he could scarcely recognize himself. He knew he'd done everything she recited now, but it seemed like someone else had said those things, made those demands—and, in the process, cut his family into pieces.

Loud, voice ringing through the room, she gave him another sliver of hope. "But that wasn't you."

He rocked back on his heel at the force of her declaration, using the angled foot piece of his prosthesis to balance.

"That wasn't you. That was this monster created by the terrible, terrible things that had happened to you.

And I don't blame you, Nathan. That's what I need you to hear and understand. You had a life-changing event happen. The injury took so much from you without your permission. Your leg, your job, your place in life—and your family. The Nathan I know and love, the Daddy that our Katie loves—that man would never have intentionally hurt us. That Nathan was stripped from you, from us, by circumstances beyond our control." She leaned in, conviction blazing from her eyes, a look of firm determination emblazoned on her face. "I want that Nathan back."

He opened his mouth, and she shook her head, cutting him off.

"No, not what you're thinking. I know we can't go back to before your injury. But we can go forward to what we can be together. Our relationship, my love, Katie's love—none of that is dependent on you having two feet, two legs, or any single physical characteristic. It's built on the man you are inside." She thumped his chest with the back of her hand, and he took the blow, ready to take on much more than that if she needed him to. He'd take anything from her if it meant she kept talking like this, kept forgiving him when he'd said and done such inexcusable things.

"The man you are in your heart and mind, that's what I want back. You told me a few minutes ago that you love me. Is that really true?"

He nodded quickly, not caring what it said that a deep sense of relief drove the motion.

"Well, I love you, too. So much, Nathan." Her face softened, eyes warming as she stared at him. "You want to know why I'm here?"

"Christmas?"

She rolled her eyes, and he swallowed, suddenly terrified. If she wasn't just here for the holidays, then that might open the door to what he wanted most in the world. He needed his family, but he needed the brotherhood he'd found in the club, too. "Why are you here, Cath? If not for Christmas, then why?"

"I want my family back." He nearly shouted with joy at her words but held back, still not believing. "I'm willing to work to make it happen. Willing to do whatever it takes. You like what you're building here?"

He stared at her, then gave a slow, single nod, hoping she'd understand that it hadn't been about doing it without her but that the club gave him something he couldn't do without. "Like's an understatement."

"I get that, and after being here just the little time I have been, I see how much it matters. That's fine. I think that's something that's outside the us I want back."

"How did I get so lucky?" Rocked by the roller coaster of emotions, he shook his head as he pulled her a little closer. "I don't deserve you."

"I don't deserve you." She repeated his words back to him immediately, and they struck deep because she was right.

"You're right. You do deserve so much more."

She rolled her eyes again, that expression somehow managing to convey irritation and amusement. "God, you're so dense sometimes. I didn't mean it that way. I meant it how you said it to me. The same, Nathan, *the same*. I don't feel like I've done enough good in the world to deserve to have you in my life. That's what I meant, not that I felt like you were a burden. You're not, never have been." She laughed, but the sound of it was wet, thick, and he knew she was close to tears. "Oh, you've been a pain in my ass sometimes, but you're *my* pain in the ass. No one else's."

"You still want me? All of that, and you aren't kickin' me to the curb?" Although she tried to blink it away, from this close, he could see the welling moisture in her eyes. "I don't want to hurt you, Cath."

"Then let's figure this out together." Her chin lifted a fraction of an inch higher. "You and me, just like it's always been."

"You and me." He glanced around the room, ultra-conscious of the sideways glances from the men. Dana was staring unabashedly, even offering him a grin and a tiny wave when he looked at her. "You hungry, or you up for getting out of here?"

"Let's go talk somewhere private. You said you can go a few blocks without too much trouble?" He nodded, gaze focused on her. She smiled and rested her palm on his chest. "Then let me show you where Katie and I are staying for this week."

"A week?" His heart leapt in his chest. Not a day, not even a couple of days, which was all he'd allowed himself to hope for when he'd granted the thought enough space in his head. A week was outside of anything he could have dared dream, and the way things were going on day one, it boded well for him. "I get you for a week?"

"Yeah, then I've got work and Katie has preschool." She paused, then the tips of her ears blushed when she said, "We should make the most of it."

"I've got the kiddo," Dana called, followed by a growling chorus of men's voices offering the same assistance.

There was a tug at his pant leg, and he looked down into Katie's eyes. "How about you, punkin? You think Daddy should walk Mommy back to the little house?"

Her nose crinkled. "Do I hafta go, too? Mr. Oscar said he's got vibeo games."

"Video," Cathy prompted, and Katie nodded in agreement.

"Vibeo." Her eyes grew round. "Do you need me to help you with the thingies?"

Nathan shook his head. "No, sweetheart. Daddy can manage the crutches without you this once. You want to stay here, then?"

"Oh, yes." Katie cut her gaze up to Cathy's face. "Is that okay, Mommy?"

"Yeah, baby. That's fine. We're not going far." Nathan looked at her to find Cathy was studiously staring elsewhere. "You sure you're okay here?"

"I promise we'll take good care of her." Kirby walked up beside Nathan. "Katie, do you remember how to pinkie promise?" She nodded eagerly. "Okay, I want you to pinkie promise me you'll be a good girl, and then I'll pinkie promise Mommy that you'll be safe here." He held out his hand, and Nathan choked up unexpectedly at the sight of his little girl reaching up to grasp Kirby's smallest finger with her own, curling her tender flesh around that scarred and rough digit easily four times the size of hers.

"I promise."

The words echoed through him, shredding his confidence with the thoughts they stirred.

I promised so many things.

Promised to be a good husband, and he'd failed miserably. Promised to keep his little girl happy, and she'd already cried today. Promised to protect and serve, and instead had wound up crippled and useless.

A familiar wave of darkness rolled over him, and Nathan turned away from the scene, grabbed the crutches, and shoved them underneath his arms. He'd known it was too good to be true. *I was right all along. Cathy would be better off without me.* He rocked his way to the front door, and without waiting, lurched through it, slapping the outside door closed behind him with a brusque movement. *Whole world would be better off.* Navigating the steps one at a time, crutches and bad leg first, then the rest of him, until, hunched over like a bell ringer, he got to the sidewalk and realized he didn't know which direction to go.

"*Fuck.*"

"What's wrong?" Cathy skipped down the stairs, navigating them nimbly, surefooted on the broad steps.

"Nothing." He swallowed the rest of what he wanted to say and stared at the concrete underneath his feet. *Foot.* "Where's this guest house?" It was safer to set things up for how he expected them to go. No matter what had been said so far, he knew better than to think Cathy had come all this way for the possibility of a reunion. Guest house, not a home. Not something he could share with her and Katie. Blackness swirled around his thoughts. *She's probably got divorce papers in her suitcase, ready for my signature.*

Her eyes narrowed and she frowned, then lifted her chin, and he nearly swung her into his arms right there. That woman staring at him was his Cath, the one he'd expected to spend the rest of his days adoring.

"Left one block, then left again, two blocks." She didn't move, holding her position on the bottom step, still just shorter than he was. "And whatever that was in there"—she gestured behind her to the closed door, the house lit with Christmas lights, now dim in the day's sunshine—"it wasn't nothing. But I want you to tell me in your own time, so I'll let it slide for now." She stepped down, took a few strides, and then turned to look where he still stood in his tracks. "Are you coming with me?"

He took her in, standing there with a fierce expression etched on her face, as if she were a warrior ready for a battle. This wasn't a woman who was willing to throw in the towel. She might have been taken off guard inside, that unbalanced moment gifting him a glimpse of the softer side of his Cath. Through the years he'd watched her change personas as needed, going from pleasant to sweet, determined and strong. He'd seen her hurt and confused, backing away from the venom spewing from his mouth, retreating. He should have known it wasn't a real withdrawal. No, Cath might have needed a few months to gather herself, but so had he.

She swallowed, and he watched the muscles in her throat move in that surrender to whatever nerves she held at bay. Her eyes softened, and before she could say anything else, he pulled himself upright, no longer leaning on the crutches. "Yeah, Cath. Yeah, sure. I'm with you."

"You don't get to do that, Nathan Smith." She advanced on him, covering the few paces between them quickly. He didn't flinch when she slapped him hard in the chest. "You don't get to be mine, and then gone, and then pretend to want to be mine again." She poked him. "You don't get to give me all of you, and make me love you, and then take yourself away from me and Katie. You wanna know why I'm here, today? Do you?"

He nodded, slowly dipping his chin toward his throat. He knew, but he still needed to hear it.

She didn't disappoint, her tone steely and certain as she told him, "I'm here because I love you. I love you and I want you in my life. In mine and Katie's lives. I want you to pick us."

"It's dark in my head sometimes, Cath." That was more than he'd admitted to anyone. How the depression could overrun his thoughts until all he could see was a final ending to everything. How it hurt so badly to know how he'd fucked up and the only thing he could think of was making that torture stop. How the phantom pain fucked with him and fucked with him until he'd try to stand on the damn leg, since if it hurt so much, if the burn was so real, how could it not be there for him anymore?

"Then let me in, baby. Let me in, because you can't do this alone." She gestured towards the building behind them. "I know you're not alone. You've got all those men who have your back, and there's a bond there that even a blind woman could see. They know, on a level I can't fathom, what you're going through." She spread her palm on his chest, and the heat from her touch grounded him, centered Nathan in a way he hadn't known he needed. "But I know you, and I know us, and I have a place in this. They have your back, that's their place. Mine?" Her chin lifted, and she stared into his eyes. "Mine is at your side. If it's dark, then let me in, and I'll spread light so far and wide you won't remember what that darkness looked like. Let me in, Nathan." Breath puffed from her mouth in tiny clouds, and her lips trembled when she added a single word. "Please."

"I don't want to lose you." She stared at him, her gaze evading interpretation, even when he needed to know what she was thinking in this moment. He laid bare his fears. "I don't want to lose Katie-bug. To lose us. I've *missed* us. I don't want to lose everything, Cath."

"Then don't." She stated this as if it were that simple. As if he could just choose to turn off the pain.

"I wanna tell you...things." Unpleasant things. Things she'd never heard him discuss. A conversation they should have had after his first deployment, or his second. A story about the man he'd had to become while on enemy soil, parts of that alternate personality having come home to roost as lasting changes to the man she'd married.

"I'm not some shrinking flower, Nathan. You should know that. If you want to talk—" She stepped to the side and looped her fingers around his wrist, as close to a handhold as they could manage while he crutched along. "—then I want to listen. You want me to get your coat?" He shook his head, spellbound by the look on her face. "Okay, then. Let's go."

They moved up the sidewalk without speaking, the click and groan of the crutches a muted addition to the near-silent day. It shouldn't be surprising that the tiny town was quiet this early on Christmas morning. Kids would still be happy to play with their presents or the boxes they came in, and parents wouldn't yet be tired of the noise and activity. Nathan supposed the story would be different in a couple of hours, families spilling outside to wear off sugar-fed energy and holiday excitement.

Right now, however, it was so quiet he could hear blood pounding inside his own head, the low-level headache that never seemed to go away steadily beating at his skull.

The house where Cathy paused was set back from the street, with just enough front yard to feel slightly isolated from the neighbors on either side. It was a single story, and he noticed the doors were wider than normal, which meant it had been modified to be accessible. "Oscar bought this?" She cut a glance over her shoulder at him as she fit a key to the lock and shrugged. "It's nice."

"Yeah, it is."

Bland conversation to get them over the threshold and shut away from the rest of the world. He had to have a barrier of some kind to be able to do to her what he needed, because Nathan knew telling her the many truths he held close to his chest would tear her down. His confessions needed privacy, and this little house offered exactly that.

The front door opened into the dining room, and he looked around as she walked through and led him farther into the house. With every step, he found another thing to like about this place. Every detail of the living room was just one more thing that told him it could be a home. Shaking his head, he reminded himself that Cathy's family and job were both back on the coast, not in bumfuck Texas.

"You want anything to drink before we settle in?" Cathy knew him, and he loved that tiny burst of remembered intimacy, the fact she'd understood how once he started talking, he wouldn't want to stop until it was all out there and transparently visible for her to see. "I'm going to grab a bottle of water. You want one, or something stronger?'

"Water'd be good." He clipped off the rest of what he'd been about to say, then shook his head at himself and forced the words out. "Liquor doesn't go well with the meds."

"Water it is." She breezed out of the room as if him admitting he'd had to resort to medication wasn't a huge announcement.

Maybe it's not. He lifted his chin. *Maybe my stubbornness taking a backseat to becoming healthier is the bigger deal*. He shook his head. It couldn't be that simple.

A bottle of water smacked down on the table beside the couch, and he watched as Cathy took a chair at right angles to the piece of furniture she evidently expected him to claim. She opened her water and took a slow drink, then stood and shrugged out of her coat and reclaimed her seat. He watched as she worked with the lid again, taking another extended sip. She stood again suddenly, closing and settling the bottle on a different table before swirling out of the room without a word.

Back at his side in a moment, she had a blanket in her hands. Walking in front of him, she gestured towards the couch. "Sit, Nathan." He looked at the couch and out of habit evaluated the height, a little surprised when it was the same kind they had at the clubhouse. Taller than normal, with firm cushions, it was an easy piece of furniture to climb off with a prosthetic. A glance at the chair told him it wasn't the same and would have been a challenge to vacate. *How could she know that?* He shook his head, and she made an impatient noise. "Please, Nathan. You're chilled through. And I…" She trailed off for a moment, but before he could explain the headshake, she picked up the conversation. "I want to sit with you. Can I?" Her gaze lifted and met his with a weight that could have staggered him backwards. Pain and hope, and the softness she'd only ever had for him.

Wordlessly, he shuffled around until he could lower himself to the cushions, depositing the crutches and tucking them alongside the furniture so they'd be out of the way. The flames curled down his thigh and around his calf, burning deep into nonexistent muscles until he must have groaned, because Cathy asked, "What's wrong?"

"I fell earlier." In case she hadn't seen how he'd deposited himself on the floor, this would give her an inkling of what his world was like now. The man who previously could run twenty clicks with a full pack on his sweating back was gone with the wind, leaving him stumbling along in the acrid wake of loss. "In doing so, I jammed the socket up on my stubbie. Somehow that jammed the lock pin. I haven't used the leg much since, but even a little use without the proper vacuum seal is enough to irritate the skin." He shrugged and turned his head. Water in hand, he spoke to the far wall. "It's not a big deal."

"Why didn't you take the leg off?" She settled onto the couch, her back angled against the far arm, legs folded and curled underneath her. The blanket was tucked around her waist, draped over the space between them.

He was struck by another wave of nostalgia and longing. They'd often sat like this, before. Watching TV and playing footsies under the cover, close enough for him to steal a kiss with every commercial break. They'd always end up those evenings with Cathy sprawled out over his legs, head cradled in the crook of his arm as he watched her sleep. Then he'd wake her gently, guide her sweetly-drowsy, half-aware self into their bedroom and help her undress for bed. By the time he had her naked, she'd be wide awake again and ready to love on him.

"It wasn't a good time to deal with it." He turned to face her, doing his best to ignore the phantom pain.

"I don't remember you being a liar." She said this so quietly, with no specific inflection, that he nearly questioned her, thinking he'd misheard. "Nathan, tell me why."

"Because I didn't want Katie to see, okay?" He jerked his head to the side, studying the curly ornamentation around a sconce on the wall. "I didn't want you to see."

"Is that why you tried to run me off from the hospital?"

"Worked, didn't it? You left and didn't come back." There were some antique-looking sepia-toned portraits on the wall, and he frowned because one of them was very familiar. "Is that my grandparents?"

"Probably." She drank from her water. "I sent some things for Oscar to use here."

Nathan studied her carefully. She was too calm, too collected. Together after months apart, she should still be raging at him. Instead she...what? Walked with him, doing as much as she could to settle him, even creating this false sense of intimacy by setting a scene certain to stir up old memories. *Why is she really here?*

He took a page from her book of stalling tactics and sipped from his water, looking around the room.

Everywhere his gaze landed, he found something familiar. A painting they'd bought while wandering around at an artist market, both of them loving the crazy depiction of a cat driving a cab. There was a desk along one wall; made from dark wood, it looked suspiciously like the one passed down to Cathy from her grandfather. More photos of family and friends, his squad. There was even one of—

"Is that my ceremony?" He tipped his chin, then lifted the bottle to point. "How did you get that?"

She twisted to look at the framed image of him on a stage, ass in a wheelchair since he hadn't been approved to walk yet, taking a thin case from a man in a suit. "I was there." Cathy looked at him, resting her chin on her shoulder. "You didn't expect me to stay away just because you told me to, did you?"

"Did Katie...was she..." He scratched at his chin fiercely, feeling the burn of raised welts his nails left behind. "Did you bring her?"

"No." She shook her head, the movement slow and somehow sorrowful. "If she'd been older, and understood what it was, I would have. If she could know what you'd sacrificed for us, I would have. But it was easier to leave her with daycare and just come by myself." She scrunched her nose. "Coward's way out, I know."

"No, it was loud and crowded. She wouldn't have had a good time." Reaching and stretching towards her, he threaded his hand underneath the cover and trailed a finger along her leg. "Thank you." He made another pass with his finger, tracing a line along her shinbone. "For coming, even after I'd been a dick to you. It means a lot."

"Why did you mail it to me?"

He stared at her, confused. His brain was lost in the feeling of touching her, the heat from their bodies making the hidden space underneath the blanket feel safe.

"Nathan? Why did you send it home, if you weren't coming back?"

"Oh." He sat back and brought his hand up, placing it on top of the blanket, palm spread over his thigh. He vaguely remembered mailing it, taking the box to the post office and begging a few pieces of tape to seal the package.

Hands shaking, he scrawled Cathy's name on the flat rate envelope, followed by the address he knew by heart. He stared at the words and markings for a moment, then added "For Katie" almost as an afterthought, crowding it in at an angle beside Cathy's name.

The chill morning didn't have anything on the cold lump in his stomach. He'd been out all day, riding by himself, loosely aiming towards a charity donor for a late afternoon pickup. Not that he'd tried hard, but not being able to talk anyone into joining him had really been freeing.

He walked to the counter and dropped the envelope on the scale, waited forever for the clerk to punch in all the information, and paid his money. Only after the package had been swept away and into a bin in the back did it dawn on him to put a letter inside, a note even. His brain soothed him. Cath would understand.

He straddled the bike and scowled down at the gauges as he tugged on his gloves. Back on the road, he hadn't gone more than five miles when he saw a bar, neon lights blazing in every window. A sign bolted to the outside wall proclaimed, "Breakfast is served," and by the smell coming from the building, they weren't lying. The scent of crisply fried bacon wafted through the air.

Once inside, he sized up the customers, slotting each group into tidy little columns in his head. The old farmers held court at a big round table in the corner, mugs of coffee in front of each. The semi parked alongside the road belonged to the man at one end of the bar, smiling at and chatting up the bartender as she washed glasses with rhythmic movements that set her tits jostling around inside her loose shirt. The other two bikes outside belonged to the black-jacketed duo straddling stools on the other end of the bar, beers and empty highball glasses within easy reach.

No real choice then, because like called to like. He left a stool between himself and the other men. The bartender walked his way, and the closer she got, the younger she looked, until he wasn't certain she could even be old enough to work behind the pine this way. He pointed at the bottles and glasses and, pushing down the advice of the doctors, said, "I'll have one of those, darlin'." She smiled and set a glass on the bar top as she slammed open a cooler, then brought out a beer with one hand, the other gripping and tilting a bottle, metal spout glugging quietly as she poured.

"Be eight bucks." She slid the beer onto a coaster already lying in front of him.

He pulled out his wallet, fishing around for a couple of bills. He handed her one and laid the other next to the beer. Lifting his glass of whiskey as she walked to get his change, he tipped it towards the bikers. "Mornin'," he offered, taking a healthy swallow. "Colder than a witch's tit out there."

Laughter and returned salutes set him at ease, and for the next hour, the three of them traded stories, Army versus Navy, all branches versus the Marines, and finally club versus club, since they were patched into a national MC. He'd gotten comfortable, and in doing so, became comfortably numb. Fuckin' finally.

"I'm Donald," a man said, interrupting the story Nathan was currently screwing up telling. He'd relayed the punch line twice now and kept having to circle back around for the setup. Donald held out a hand. "And you are?"

Narrowing his eyes, he reached out and gripped the man's hand, taking his stance behind the bar as someone with an official standing here. Nathan glanced up at the clock to see it was just gone eleven o'clock. He shook his head as he responded, "Nathan. Pleased ta meet cha."

"Nathan, you're drunk in my bar on a weekday, and it ain't even afternoon yet." Donald gripped tighter. "You and me, we're gonna set this to rights. Faye," he called over his shoulder towards the little bartender Nathan realized had stopped coming his direction a while ago, the empty state of his glass and bottle testimony to her attempts at slowing him down. "Bring me a couple of coffees, yeah?" She nodded nervously, and Nathan wondered if he'd gotten her in trouble. "Get an order in for my good friend Nathan here, tell Jimmy to make a boatload of fries, the greasier the better, then smother 'em with gravy."

"Thanks, Don," one of the bikers said, standing and shrugging on his jacket. "Sounds like you got this handled." The other man stood too, yanking on his gloves. With a lifted hand to Nathan, they made their

way outside, and he heard the unmistakable rumble of pipes as they started their bikes.

He looked back at this man, this Don, who'd walked in and run off his friends. "What's happening?"

Don swung around the end of the bar and laid claim to the stool closest to Nathan. "What's happening is you're drunk in my bar, and my friends called me about you. See, they said you sounded like you wanted to do something stupid and were on a bike." He pushed a mug of coffee closer.

Nathan stared at it, confused. He hadn't seen Faye drop it off, focused as he'd been on Don.

"I've lost friends to wrecks over the years and wished I could have done something for them. Family and friends, and I've lost customers, too. I didn't feel like dealing with the shit that comes with all of it. Not today. ATF all up in our shit about serving a man lying dead in a bloody pile on the road." Don shook his head. "Not today. If you're gonna do something stupid, then you'll pick somewhere else to launch from."

Nathan stared at him, not finding it in himself to deny the pull of the promised peace.

Sure, the idea was almost always there, hovering in the back of his mind, a viper just waiting for an opening. But Nathan didn't give it the time of day. He kept his shit tight and right, and kept it at bay. "What did I say?"

"You that drunk you don't know?" Don's gaze was heavy, piercing through Nathan even as it held him in place. "You told Faye it was your little girl's birthday yesterday, and you didn't call. Didn't see her. Said it would be better if she never saw you again. Then you gave sweet Faye all the money in your possession, said you didn't need it anymore." Don's head swung back and forth slowly. "If that ain't a cry for help, I don't know what one is, brother."

"I—" Almost he said he wouldn't, couldn't have told the little bartender those things, but a memory, already fading, told him maybe he would. Maybe he already had. "I love my little girl."

"I do not doubt that, man. No doubts. But life, she can suck balls sometimes." A pause, then Don asked the most intrusive question Nathan hated to answer. Strangers feeling they could own a little piece of him, taking his service and sacrifice and changing it into something they merged with their own lives and expectations. "Where'd you serve?"

Nathan stared at the man, noting for the first time the tidy haircut. High and tight, and dusted with gray, testimony to a life well lived. Nathan saw the well-known insignia inked into the muscles and skin of Don's forearm, flexing underneath the art as he lifted the coffee. Military knew military, always. It didn't matter if their service had been separated by decades and delivered on different foreign lands. Military knew military.

A couple of hours passed then, as they talked about their jobs, their squads, their families. Don had a shrapnel wound in his bicep that had taken the service unexpectedly, much as the loss of Nathan's leg had *ripped it away from him. By three o'clock, Nathan was sober and ready to climb back on the bike. He still had the meat of the run ahead of him, traveling one town over to pick up a donation check for the club and foundation.*

Don walked outside with him and stopped with his hand on Nathan's shoulder. Nathan turned at the touch, staring into the face of this unexpected friend.

"Son, if you ever find yourself in that place again..." Don paused, and Nathan knew he wasn't talking about the bar they'd just exited, but the dark state of mind Nathan carried around. "Give me a call. Don't do anything stupid." A squeeze and a wave, and the door closed behind him.

Nathan stared at the bar for a minute, feeling better than he had in a while. Might be time to come clean to Kirby and Oscar about where his head was. Circle the wagons, because he knew all he had to do was mention the emotions swamping his mind and they'd be on him like flies on shit. Invasive as hell, but that was why they had such a good success rate. Intensive involvement, aggressive intervention, and determined support.

No matter his mind was tangled up in the past, ideas shooting through his head as fast as his brain could conjure them, like the bullets from a gun set on a hill to make a stand. Mad minute, it was called, where the gunner let loose, sixty seconds of unrelenting assault to clear the way for friendlies to do what was needed. Either advance or retreat. "I need a mad minute."

Kirby would know what he meant. All he had to do was say so.

"Nathan?" Cathy's voice sounded flat, far away. "Baby?"

He blinked.

Her hands rested on him, palm to skin, fingers tracing tiny pathways along the ridges of clenched muscles. Nathan turned his head and saw fear on her face—not for herself; this was sorrow mixed with terror, and he knew he'd caused that look. "I wasn't going to come home."

She froze for a split second, a stutter of movement he would have missed if he weren't focusing a hundred percent of his attention on her. She hadn't expected honesty from him, and that hurt. "Okay." Her tongue swept out and across her bottom lip, and he wanted to capture it with his mouth, wanted to know if she still had any desire for his touch, his kisses. "What were you going to do?"

"Stay here, long as I could." He leaned back against the couch, comforted when she eased closer. "Was gonna stay until I couldn't anymore."

"And now?"

She'd asked the thousand-dollar question of the week. Maybe the year. "I know you gotta go back. There's work and school, and everything. House." She didn't respond to any of his prompts, and he remembered his thoughts of her coming here to seek a divorce, something to finalize the unwilling limbo he'd forced her into by leaving as he had. "So, you don't want a…divorce, make it legal or something? Really?"

"What?" The shock was real, unfeigned, and he sagged in relief. "No, Nathan. No."

"I can't go back, Cath." He shook his head. "Every part of our lives back there is wound up in the man I used to be, and when I'm there, that's all I see. Then versus now. And, baby, the differences are haunting. Here—" He gestured back towards the street, in the direction where the clubhouse stood. "I can be me. The one I am now."

"You're still both of those, Nathan. In my eyes, there are no differences between then and now, but I think…I think I understand." When she looked at him this time, it was with glinting wetness in her eyes, and a hopeful upwards tilt of her lips. "No, I know I do. I understand." She touched his face, the caress gentle and soft. He closed his eyes as her fingers trailed along his jaw. "I understand."

"I fuckin' love you." Nathan twisted to face her and reached out, fingers digging into her hips as he pulled her into his lap. She adjusted, slung a leg across his thighs and straddled him, holding herself slightly off his legs. "Do you love me? Can you still love me, like this?"

She didn't answer him with words, left them both in an oasis of quiet. Instead, she leaned close and pressed her mouth to his. Chaste and soft, this wasn't a lead-in for romance but an effective affirmation of the nonverbal kind. Nathan gave himself over to it, the tip of his tongue tracing along her lips in his own silent request, and she opened so sweetly he groaned, long and low. Hands on his shoulders, she met him kiss for kiss, until they were both breathing heavily. He broke away and stared at her, the flush of arousal giving her face color. Her eyes were dark, pupils blown with desire.

"This place got a bedroom?" Her lips bowed when she gasped at the question, a surprised intake of breath that told him she was entirely onboard with the idea. "There's never been anybody for me but you, Cath. Always you." He tightened his fingers, holding fast to her, letting the knowledge bolster his courage that she might love him still. "If you want me, still want me, that is."

"You silly, silly man." She kissed him again, this time leading with hot and wet action, their tongues twisting and stroking, teeth biting gently. She pulled back, then kissed along his jaw until she was whispering into his ear. "Always and forever, my love. I want you more than you can know."

He remained still while she climbed off him, her every movement sinuous and sensual. Then she turned all business as she leaned down, fingers grasping his belt. She braced and out of habit, he put his hands on her shoulders, ready to balance himself. "On three," she muttered, then counted down. The height of the couch worked in their favor, but she conducted the lift as smoothly as Oscar could have. A moment later and he was balanced on his good leg, thigh muscles complaining. Crutches retrieved, he nodded at her.

"Lead the way, beautiful."

"I love that. I don't think I ever told you, but when you call me beautiful like it's my name? I love that, handsome."

"Same, baby. Same." Crutch wedged under his arm, he reached out and gripped the back of her neck to pull her close for another kiss. He whispered, "Show me the bedroom," against her mouth and felt her quiver. "Come on, baby, light my fire."

"You're so cheesy." She was laughing now, which was his intent, because he had to slow them down a little. There were things to discuss before he'd be sleeping with his wife, and even as he mentally acknowledged the reality, he knew how fucked up that was, since there had been months and months to get it right and he'd been a coward and run, fled into the middle of the country, leaving her hanging on behind him, making her responsible for their whole lives even as he abandoned her.

The therapist had used the term self-loathing during a session. It'd been one single time the man had slipped up, mentioning how hard Nathan was on himself, and he'd latched on to the word. He did loathe himself, because there were so many ways he could have reacted to what had happened, to losing his leg, to having his brains scrambled—and none of that shitty talk about how that exempted him from being responsible for his own actions. Nathan was a fan of owning your mistakes, and so many months ago, he'd made the biggest mistake of his life.

He followed her up the hallway, seeing more homey touches everywhere he looked. They passed the room Katie slept in, and he stopped short, looking around at the princess theme. "Looks like something pink exploded."

Cathy came back and stood next to him, laughing softly. "Oscar didn't know what else to do with it, I think."

"Seems a lot of work to go to for a weeklong visit." Her laughter trailed off, and he thought again about all the small personal touches he'd already seen. "It's not really just a visit, is it?"

"Nathan—"

"Tell me, Cath." He didn't turn, kept his eyes on the room his daughter would sleep in tonight, and the next. There was a picture on the nightstand, him holding her in his lap. From here he couldn't see the wheelchair he knew was there and couldn't remember Cathy ever having a camera the couple of times he'd allowed them to visit him in rehab. Katie was smiling at him, hand on either cheek as she smushed his face for a kiss. The absolute joy in his daughter's face caught at his breath, and he ground out the demand again. "Tell me I get to keep you."

"I want my family. Katie wants her dad. And I know, deep in my gut, Nathan, I know you want us, too." Her voice quavered, and he dropped his weight onto a crutch for support as he reached out for her hand. Cathy's fingers were tight around his, cold as ice and trembling. "I wanted to wait to tell you, to make sure you would be okay with it, but we're set to move here at spring break. My job's willing to let me work remotely, with just a couple of trips a year back to the main office. There's a good school here in Mayhan, and Katie? She just wants to be where you are. Where we both are."

The barest glimmer of hope that he could have everything made his throat tight, and he blinked away any evidence of moisture before he turned to face her.

Nathan nearly strangled on the words but pushed through because he *needed* to know. "You heard me earlier, right?" She nodded. "You know what it means, all of it? You heard—" He paused a moment and gulped desperately at the choking knot in his throat. "You heard it all, right?"

"Nathan." Her eyes swept closed, and she pulled in a shallow, quick breath. "I heard everything you said, every word. I heard all that, and the things you didn't." She took a step backwards, and his heart stuttered in his chest, thinking it a retreat. Then she smiled, and it felt as if the sun had broken through the clouds overhead, beaming down on him. "I heard your love, and your fear." Shadows crawled over her face, but then that smile blanketed him again. "I'm choosing to hang on to that love, Nathan. I want to hold tight to that, want to use it to wedge my way back into your heart, your life. I want you. I've missed you." Her voice broke, cracked through the middle, then firmed back up as she visibly pulled herself together to finish. "Missed you so much. You've missed us, too. And just you saying that tells me that this is the first step back to where we need to be. This, you and me, right here, this is us choosing each other and choosing to move forwards. This is us picking us." She held out her hand, fingers curled in invitation. "Pick us, babe. I will upend our world if I get a chance to rebuild it with you. Gladly move across the country if it means we're together. I've done it before." He nodded. She had, too many times. Him in the field and her handling the whole shebang. "We're here for a week, then gone for about eight. Can you wait that long to be us again?"

"Oh fuck no." He swept the crutches in front of him, and now she was moving faster, leading the way towards the bedroom. Nathan pursued her, body swinging in an arc as he tracked his willing prey until they were in the bedroom and she was poised in front of him, eyes shining with so much love.

Standing close to her, he rested one crutch against the edge of the bed and leaned in, cupping her cheek in his palm. "I want us." He kissed her, lips moving across hers softly. "Want us, so much." Her fingers circled his wrist, holding him steady. She'd always been there for him in every way. "I don't..." He paused for a breath, then finished, "I don't want to disappoint."

"You. Oh, you. My Nathan. You'd never, ever disappoint." She shifted against him, lithe body pressed tight to his. "I want only what you can give." Her fingertips scratched aimless patterns through his hair, nails dragging against his scalp, something he'd loved, something she'd always done, something he hadn't realized he'd missed like fuck until he had it back. Like everything else about her, the memories of how good they were together had been stuffed deep into a dark corner of his mind. "The most important part of anything that happens between us is it's you and me. Us." She offered her lips again, and he took them harshly, with bruising force, stirring sweet moans from her throat. "Us."

"I'll need a minute," he whispered against the column of her throat. "There's prep time we didn't have before." She hummed soft and low, the sound stirring through his cock, providing an unexpected stiffening and shifting against the loose pants he wore. *Maybe not so much prep as I thought.* "And I don't want to put a damper on this." He slipped his hand across her belly, catching and caressing her breast, lifting and plumping the flesh. "But there are parts of me that won't look the same."

"Nathan Smith," she mock growled, running her teeth along the edge of his jaw. "You think I'm only in this for your looks?" The laugh she gave was light, trilling with humor, and bright with love. "While on the outside you are the handsomest man I know"—he endured an eternity waiting, and she gave it to him with another nip, another sweet kiss—"I'm all about how you are inside."

"How am I inside?" With his crutch wedged into his pit, his fingertips found a way under her shirt, and he curved around to pluck at the fastening on her bra. Restricting clothing loosened, he tweaked and pinched her nipple into a hard bud, peaked and ready for his mouth. "What do you see when you look at me?" Face dipping to her chest, he nuzzled her shirt up so his mouth was against her skin and he could draw her deep, flicking the hardened nipple with his tongue, laving softly across the puckered flesh. "What do you see, baby?"

Hands gentle as she cradled his skull, she held him to her breasts, back arching as she offered herself to him, moaning softly when he suckled hard. "I see the man I married." A flick followed by a gentle bite set another moan free, and he smiled against her skin. "The man I love. I see the man I chose to create another human with." Nathan breathed in the scent of her, the woman he'd known for years, the aroma of her arousal something he'd missed. His brain had recognized her even before his body, back at the clubhouse, the pattern of her indelibly etched on him.

He matched the crutches together and shoved them under the bed, pivoted on his good foot until his ass was against the mattress, and sighed in relief as Cathy slipped between his thighs. She pressed close, as if she'd never been absent from his life.

"I love you." He cupped her jaw in both hands, pulling her in for a kiss. Her lips had shed any chill from the outdoors and were warm and supple underneath his mouth. Again and again, he kissed her, working side to side, then focusing on her full bottom lip, plucking and nibbling until he drew gasps and moans from her. His words were punctuation for each caress, tokens of love and faith spoken for her ears only.

His arms lifted at her urging, and his shirt joined the crutches on the floor. Cathy's fingertips trawled lines across his chest and shoulders, drawing strands of fire along his tattoos and scars, but this fire left him hard and aching instead of groaning in pain. "You're real, Cath. Really, really here."

"I'm here, babe, always will be. There's nowhere else I want to be." Hot and wet, her mouth moved across his chest, teeth dragging a rough path over his nipples. "Always you." Her clothing floated through the air, both of their hands in constant movement. Connecting, reassuring, arousing.

The clink of his belt buckle broke the bubble surrounding them. He covered her hands with his. "Hold, Cath. I want to."

"I've seen, Nathan. I'm not afraid of what happened to you. I've seen, and I still love you." Her head lifted, fingers threading between his as their gazes locked. "I'm not afraid."

"Maybe I am." Nathan struggled to control his breathing, suddenly deep and quick as if he'd run blocks at a sprint, something he wasn't able to do anymore, but he could sure fuck things up fast. "Maybe I am, Cath. I don't want..." Her head swung back and forth slowly. "You gotta just...give me a minute."

"I've read about the surgeries, Nathan. I know what happened. What you've endured."

"That's...clinical. Not the reality that I live with every day." He blew out a shaking breath. "I wanna show you my way." She gave his hands a squeeze and nodded, standing nude in front of him. He let his gaze map her stunning curves, each inch of exquisite flesh so well known. "You're gorgeous, baby. Gorgeous. My beautiful wife." She shrugged, and he dipped his head, lapping at her nipple. "I want you." His dick gave a twitch behind a still-closed zipper. "So fucking much."

She stared at him, and her eyes narrowed, giving her an uncertain look for only a moment. Then Cathy stepped away, holding onto his fingers until they no longer reached. Circling around him, she flipped back the covers and settled in the center of the mattress. Arms lifted, palms crossed underneath her head, she studied him with a calm, steady gaze. "Show me."

Confidently on display like that, unafraid of what he'd say or think, no matter they'd been apart for months, she was modeling the kind of courage he'd need to get through the next few minutes. "Woman, you humble me."

"No, babe. I love you."

With a deep breath, he pushed off the edge of the mattress and stood, back to her. She'd already been seeing the evidence of that last mission, that last route walked with his brothers. Shrapnel had shredded his upper back while he'd been crumpled over the fender of the Stryker, pinned to the wall, blasting through his tissue when an RPG hit the top of the building directly behind him.

He listened carefully, but her breathing didn't change, didn't vary. He bent double, worked to grip the sock covering his lower limb inside the socket between his fingers, and pulled tautly. Holding it there, he let go with one hand and used a fingertip to depress the lock pin. The familiar vacuum released its hold on his leg, and he pushed, letting the leg fall away. Balancing easily on his remaining leg, he slipped the sleeve down and off, drawing it right-side out by habit. He draped it across the prosthesis and shoved both underneath the bed, alongside the crutches.

Throat thick with terror, Nathan unbuckled his belt and shoved his pants and underwear down before he leaned back against the edge of the mattress. A coordinated rock and lift later and he was as naked as Cath. The mechanics of the process had flagged his cock's interest, and it lay semirigid along his thigh. Perfect, smooth skin contrasted with the roughened and pocked scars of his upper leg. *Cath is stronger than I am.*

Holding tight to that thought, he pushed off the mattress and stood, then pivoted awkwardly until he faced Cathy. Her gaze fixed on his face, a tiny smile curving the edges of her mouth. With a shrug, he lifted his arms out to the sides and stood, palms facing her. "This is what you're fighting for. All I am. This is what you get, Cath. Can you be happy with this?"

Her smile broadened, teeth glinting behind her plump lips. "I can get on board with what you've got to offer, Nathan." He shook his head sharply, gesturing towards his lower body. "Oh, yeah. I see you. I see you, Nathan." She shifted, sliding closer on the soft sheets, until her heel dangled off the edge of the bed next to his leg. She stretched, toes curling, and touched the largest of the scars along his outer thigh. "I see a strong man who survived something that would have killed anyone else." He closed his eyes when her gaze dipped, not wanting to see the look on her face when she saw it all.

More rustling from the sheets, closer than before. Nathan squeezed his eyes tighter, waiting.

A moment later, the noises ceased, but a supernova bloomed around his cock. He startled, nearly lurching away, but Cath's hands on his hips steadied him. Nathan stared down and watched as she fed his cock into her mouth, surrounding him with hot and wet suction. "Jesus, baby."

It didn't take a moment until he'd outgrown her ability to take him in, and her head began bobbing slowly. Just as much as the friction and suction, the heat and movement, those damn sounds Cath made as she went down on him were a turn-on for Nathan. Eager, humming her enjoyment, she gave no indication she was focused on anything other than his cock. Scars and ridges from stitches, uneven edges from skin grafts—all within inches of her face, and yet her eyes were fixed upwards, focused on his.

"I love you."

Cath pulled back, lapped at the end of his cock with the flat of her tongue for a moment, then made him groan when she sucked on the head hard, hollowing her cheeks around him. With a mischievous smile, she released him and nuzzled into the hinge of his hip. "I know you do."

"It's not going to bother you?" Her chin dipped, and he watched as she traced several of the scars. Each touch was featherlight, teasing, and soft. What it wasn't was tentative, frightened, or cautious. "You're okay with it? With me?"

"I'll never be okay with what happened to you." Anger twisted her features, and she shoved to her knees, balled fists thudding against his chest, still firm from hours and hours of PT and determination. "It took you from me for too long, Nathan. It stole from you. I'll never be okay with what happened."

The nuance of her language wormed through before he could feel terror at her words. She wasn't rejecting him, not in any way. She was rejecting what had happened, same as he had for months. But she was doing it in a healthy way, following a path that would pull them closer together, instead of driving a wedge between them as he had.

"Cath." The tremble in his voice was terrifying, something he couldn't control. Like so much of his life lately, running amok and out of control.

"I will forever be okay with *you*, Nathan." Her palms spread across his chest, curving up and over his shoulders to wind around his neck. She tugged, and he bent over her, hand to the mattress as she scooted back, leading the way. "With you." Knee between her thighs, he slipped into place on top of her as Cath settled back against the pillows.

Mouths clashed, lips caught and released in kisses that drew them together, carrying both along this river of desire he'd found only with her. Her hands clutched him close, slipping along the muscles of his upper back, skimming as he arched, cock sliding through the wetness between her legs. She puffed a breath out, hot air gusting alongside his cheek, and he moved again, twisting his hips to grind against her clit. "Cath, I want—"

"I want, too, Nathan. Oh, how I want."

Her fingers wrapped around his cock, and she directed him to her entrance, rocking her hips up to catch him on the next downward thrust, and he pushed inside, heat and wetness clasping him tightly. "Ah, God." His residual limb scraped along the sheets, but for the first time, he understood the critical importance of having his knee as he used it to spread her legs wider and anchored himself to thrust deeper. Muscles burning, the twist of his back would hurt later, but right now all he could feel was something sweet and too long gone from his life: the uncounted beauty of loving his wife.

Calves wrapped around his hips, she met him thrust for thrust, undulating in rhythm with every push. She lifted a hand and wedged it against the headboard, holding herself in place against his movements. A soft groan split the air, and he captured her mouth, tongue diving inside in time with his cock. He curled an arm around her waist, shoving far underneath until he could feel himself entering her. "Beautiful, can you? Are you close?"

"Mmhmm." Mouth closed over the arch of his shoulder, she hummed and trembled in his arms. He ground down against her, clit trapped between their bodies, and she came apart around him. Clenching tight, fluttering movements of her inner muscles pulled him deep, and Nathan held the same pace as long as he could, giving them both pleasure with every movement.

"Cath." That was all the warning he could give, the only sound he let escape, holding in the noises that wanted to beat against his throat. Deep, then deeper yet, and his cock pulsed, strikes of lightning curling around his balls and up his back, down his thighs until his toes curled into the mattress.

"I love you, Nathan Smith." Cath's murmur against his ear pricked the hair on his arms.

He kissed the side of her neck, then mouth to the curve of her cheek, gave it back to her. "I love you, Cathy Smith." They stayed like that for a minute, breathing slowing, hearts beating in time, until he promised her, "I'm keeping you."

He chuckled at his bold statement and knew she liked it when she giggled, tightening around him again. "I'm keeping you back, mister."

"You couldn't get rid of me if you tried." As close to a promise as this moment needed. "I'm not running." *Never again*.

Chapter Six
Nathan

Strolling up the sidewalk, Nathan curled Cathy closer to his side. The clubhouse loomed just ahead, only a half block away. Lights shone out the windows, creating an oasis of light and support. "So I've got you for a week, huh?"

"Yup, we don't have to leave until New Year's Day." She snuggled against his arm, crutches left behind in the house held in both of their names. He hadn't asked what magic Oscar had worked to make that happen, or how the man had managed to keep the renovation a secret, either. Not of Cathy, at least. He'd be asking Oscar face-to-face, soon.

Not today, though. This was Christmas, and magic was supposed to happen.

"You think Katie will be okay with me staying over?"

"Oh, yeah. She'll be more than okay with it." Cathy's voice bubbled with amusement. "Be ready for an early morning wake-up. She's missed that, a lot."

"Is it really this easy? Can it be this easy?" He slowed and stopped, and Cathy swung around in front of him, chin lifted as if she were ready for a fight. "No, really, Cath. How can you forgive me?"

She drew a deep breath, eyes fixed on his. Bottom lip between her teeth, she studied him seriously. "Will there be moments where I want to smack you for stealing time from me?" She shrugged, eyes bright as she blinked quickly. "Probably." A broken laugh nearly turned into something else, and he lost sight of her mouth when she covered her trembling lips with a hand. "I'm human, Nathan. You're going to irritate me, and you're going to cop attitude, and you're going to disappear inside your head and I'm going to get scared, then mad, and then who knows what." Her hand dropped, and she smiled at him, that broad beam of love only she had ever directed his way. "And none of that matters at the end of the day. Because through it all, I'll know you love me. And you'll know I love you." She thumped his chest with the palm of one hand. "And that's why it's this easy."

Behind her, the door to the clubhouse opened, and Katie darted out, connected to Kirby by his grip on her hand. In the distance, Nathan heard his best friend's voice threaded through with laughter as he called, "She's tired of waitin' on you, old man."

Cathy stepped to the side and waved in a rolling motion. "Come on down, Katie bug."

Katie was in motion almost before Kirby released his hold. She took the steps that had frustrated Nathan only hours before in two big jumps, her landing secure. She pivoted and pelted up the sidewalk, arms waving over her head. "Daddy, Daddy."

Nathan shifted his stance, centering himself before she got to him, anticipating the leap that took her up and up, at arms reach flying in the sky, then back down to be cradled against his chest. Over her head, he locked gazes with Cathy, seeing the final lines of tension fading away. "I'm right here, baby. Right here with you."

~~~

THANK YOU

Thank you so much for reading *Mad Minute*, book two in my Mayhan Bucklers MC series. These stories have a dear place in my heart, and I hope you've enjoyed it.

ABOUT THE AUTHOR

Raised in the south, MariaLisa learned about the magic of books at an early age. Every summer, she would spend hours in the local library, devouring books of every genre. Self-described as a book-a-holic, she says "I've always loved to read, but then I discovered writing, and found I adored that, too. For reading...if nothing else is available, I've been known to read the back of the cereal box."

Also by MariaLisa deMora

Alace Sweets

A dark thriller, this book is not a light read. Filled with edge-of-your-seat suspense, this intense story commands the reader's attention as it drives towards the explosive ending. Alace Sweets is a vigilante serial killer, with everything that implies and is sure to trip all your triggers. Be ready.

At seventeen, Alace Sweets turned a corner in her life, taking the wrong shortcut home from school.

Resisting the harsh knowledge her attackers will never be made to pay for their actions, Alace takes a stand. Justice must be served, and if fate's scales are out of balance, she's determined to set things right as best she can.

When the laws of men fail, the rules of Alace prevail.

5-Star Reviews for Alace Sweets

"deMora has a superb story-line and exceptional character development. All of her characters have such depth that will intrigue the reader..."
~Turning Another Page

"Hot, sweet, dark thriller."
~Beth D

"It will keep you on the edge of your seat and give you chills."
~Escape Reality Book Blog

"Disturbing, haunting, sickly; yet hot, sexy and heart racing!"
~Amanda L

"From the first page [deMora] pulls you into the world she has created and you do not even try to escape..."
~Little Shop of Readers Blog

"A must read for all those dark, gritty romance fans out there."
~Sweet & Spicy Reads

"You will find yourself so drawn into the story that the outside world is blocked out and your locking the doors and turning on all the lights."
~Danena F

"Don't judge me for bonding with a vigilante serial killer, she's more than what she does."
~iScream Books

"Thrilling...chilling...full of suspense, nail biting edge of your seat excitement."
~Tracey H

"Every time MariaLisa deMora picks up her pen (or opens her computer), she creates characters you want to believe in."
~Gail S

"Intriguing dark storyline, beautiful love story and nail-biting conclusion, what more could a reader ask for?"
~Manda M

"This book takes you a dark and twisted ride that is gripping..."
~Renee Entress' Blog

"This book is dark and gritty and I literally had to take a day off from reading it because it's that intense."
~My Girlfriend's Couch

"This is my favourite book so far from this author ... I recommend this book if you enjoy dark romantic thrillers."
~Cheekypee Reads and Reviews

"There's not enough stars to give this book and 5 just doesn't really do it justice!"
~DeLane C

"I couldn't put this book down from page one! Tried to stop & go to bed but couldn't sleep thinking about Alace and got up & finished the book."
~Debbie M

"MariaLisa DeMora, wordsmith that she is, made this a story of the enlightenment of a woman and finding love in a life where she has had none."
~Kat W

"Whatever deep dark trench [deMora] pulled a character like Alace from should be revisited again and often."
~Confessions of a Serial Reader

ADDITIONAL SERIES AND BOOKS

Please note that books in a series frequently feature characters from additional books within that series. If series books are read out of order, readers will twig to spoilers for the other books, so going back to read the skipped titles won't have the same angsty reveals.

Rebel Wayfarers MC series:

Mica, #1
A Sweet & Merry Christmas, #1.5
Slate, #2
Bear, #3
Jase, #4
Gunny, #5
Mason, #6
Hoss, #7
Harddrive Holidays, #7.5
Duck, #8
Biker Chick Campout, #8.5
Watcher, #9
A Kiss to Keep You, #9.25
Gun Totin' Annie, #9.5
Secret Santa, #9.75
Bones, #10
Gunny's Pups, #10.25
Never Settle, #10.5
Not Even A Mouse, #10.75
Fury, #11
Christmas Doings, #11.25
Gypsy's Lady, #11.5
Cassie, #12
Road Runner's Ride, #12.5

Occupy Yourself band series:

Born Into Trouble, #1
Grace In Motion, #2 (TBD)
What They Say, #3 (TBD)

Neither This, Nor That MC series:

This Is the Route Of Twisted Pain, #1
Treading the Traitor's Path: Out Bad, #2
Shelter My Heart, #3
Trapped by Fate on Reckless Roads, #4
Thunderstruck, #5

Mayhan Bucklers MC series:

Most Rikki-Tik, #1
Mad Minute, #2
Pucker Factor, #3

If You Could Change One Thing: Tangled Fates Stories

There Are Limits, #1
Rules Are Rules, #2
The Gray Zone, #3

Other Books:

With My Whole Heart
Alace Sweets
Hard Focus

More information available at mldemora.com.

www.ingramcontent.com/pod-product-compliance
Lightning Source LLC
Chambersburg PA
CBHW071233170626
46809CB00008BA/3035